# THE
# DINOSAUR
# DUSTER

For Barbara and Carol
— D. K.

For my son, David
— M. M.

Text copyright © 1992 by Donn Kushner
Illustrations copyright © 1992 by Marc Mongeau

**Canadian Cataloguing in Publication Data**

Kushner, Donn, 1927 —
The dinosaur duster

ISBN 1-895555-38-8

I. Mongeau, Marc.    II. Title.

PS8571. U84D56 1992      jC813' .54    C92-094213-X
PZ7.K85Di 1992

Lester Publishing Limited
56 The Esplanade
Toronto, Ontario
M5E 1A7

Printed and bound in China

92  93  94  95  5  4  3  2  1

# THE
# DINOSAUR
# DUSTER

### BY
## DONN KUSHNER
### PICTURES BY
## MARC MONGEAU

Of all the guards in the museum, only Mr. Mopski knew how to dust dinosaur bones properly. When he first came to the museum he was stationed by the entrance at the brass grill, which he polished until it hurt the ticket takers' eyes. He was promoted to dusting the Inuit carvings, then to the African sculpture, and finally to the museum's pride and joy: two dinosaur skeletons in the second-floor gallery, a stegosaurus in the north window and a triceratops in the south window.

Every afternoon, Mr. Mopski collected his feather duster, his mops, and his stepladder and went over each of the dinosaur skeletons, from the tip of the tail to the end of the nose, polishing every spike and plate. When he was all alone he would sing while he dusted, mostly old folk songs from his homeland amid the Carpathian Mountains which, as it happened, was the very place where the dinosaur skeletons had been found.

In a museum you can never tell who may be listening. One afternoon, while Mr. Mopski was singing "A Soldier Boy Loves Sour Cabbage," he heard a sound like a creaking iron door. A voice croaked, "That old thing again!"

"Who's that?" Mr. Mopski cried. He put down the mop with which he had been dusting the stegosaurus' bumpy tail and looked around the room.

"Don't stop," the same voice said. "It's only me."

Mr. Mopski realized with a sudden thrill that the stegosaurus was talking to him.

"I heard peasants sing that song a thousand times when I was buried in the Carpathian Mountains," said the stegosaurus.

Mr. Mopski walked to the stegosaurus' head. "I didn't know you could talk."

"I never saw the point before," answered the stegosaurus. "But go on dusting me. The tickling warms me up."

"Certainly," Mr. Mopski replied.

"Ah," the stegosaurus sighed, "that brings back memories of the old days."

"Memories?" asked Mr. Mopski, glancing at the dinosaur's empty skull.

"Our thoughts were few and simple," the stegosaurus explained. "When the rest of us died, our memories stayed with our bones."

Mr. Mopski continued dusting. "How do you like living here?" he asked finally.

"So-so," the stegosaurus told him. "I can see only the park. Nothing happens there. The tulips sprout in the spring and the leaves fall in the autumn."

"There's a couple strolling with a baby," Mr. Mopski said.

"Even they didn't stay in the park," said the stegosaurus. He sniffed. "Nó, I want excitement. If only I looked out of the south window, into the street! A city street must be such a lively place."

"The triceratops has that view," Mr. Mopski said.

"I'm well aware of that," said the stegosaurus. "Why don't you ask him how *he* likes it?"

At first, when Mr. Mopski spoke to the triceratops, the dinosaur refused to answer. Finally he growled, "That stegosaurus talks too much. Now I suppose you'll tell everyone."

"I can keep a secret," Mr. Mopski assured him. "But tell me, how do you like the view from your window?"

"It's much too busy and noisy," the triceratops complained. Several taxis sped past, and a moment later, a police car with its siren blaring.

"There they go again," the triceratops grumbled. "I never know what to expect next! The stegosaurus. . . ." He sighed. "Now there's a lucky dinosaur. He can look at the beautiful, peaceful park."

"He said he'd prefer your view," Mr. Mopski told him.

"He's welcome to it, if I could look at the park," the triceratops declared.

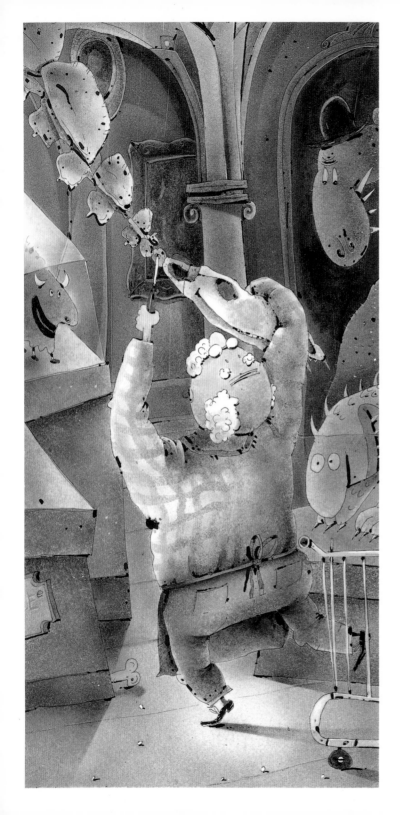

Mr. Mopski thought for a long time about what the two dinosaurs had said. He knew he could make them both happy by changing their places around. But they were much too big for him to move alone and he could hardly expect the museum officials to help him. At last he realized that if he moved only the heads of the dinosaurs, they could see out of different windows.

The stegosaurus liked the idea at once; the triceratops grumbled at first, but finally agreed.

After the museum closed, Mr. Mopski, armed with a large screwdriver, carefully unscrewed the clamps holding the skulls to the neck bones. He moved the head of the stegosaurus across from the north to the south window, and the head of the triceratops from the south to the north window. He attached the head of the stegosaurus to the body of the triceratops and the head of the triceratops to the body of the stegosaurus, clamping everything in place.

"Ah, that's better!" the stegosaurus head said.

"Let's hope it is," the triceratops head said doubtfully.

Mr. Mopski dimmed the lights. "You'll feel much better in the morning," he told the dinosaurs.

He was right. When Mr. Mopski arrived the next morning the dinosaurs were radiant.

"What excitement!" said the stegosaurus head, watching the busy street.

The triceratops head was even more pleased as it looked over the beautiful park. "What peace!" it murmured.

That same morning, however, the director of the museum brought in three visiting dinosaur experts.

"I say! What have we here?"

"*Zut alors!*"

"*Vunderbar!* What strange, never-in-this-world-before-described beasts! Where did you find them?"

The director smiled wisely. He didn't notice any change, but he didn't want to admit it. "We have our secrets," he said.

The German expert cleared his throat. "You have two new species here," he announced importantly: "A tricerosaurus *und* a stegatops!"

Then all three experts cried together, "The whole world must learn about these wonderful creatures!"

The director and his board agreed. They decided to send the dinosaurs on exhibit around the world, with Mr. Mopski as caretaker.

The tricerosaurus and the stegatops were packed into big wooden crates and loaded into an ocean liner.

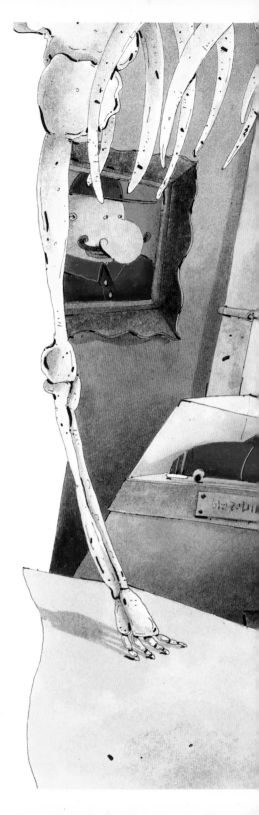

The first night at sea
Mr. Mopski could not sleep.
He put on his bathrobe and slippers
and climbed down to the ship's hold to
check on the dinosaurs.

As he approached their crates he heard the sound
of singing. The air was filled with the old Carpathian
folk song, "When Will Uncle Dimitri Finally Go to Bed?"
in the tricerosaurus' bass voice and the stegatops' tenor.

"Would you like to join in?" the tricerosaurus asked shyly.

"Certainly," said Mr. Mopski. He began the song's second verse.
They sang the next twenty-two verses together.

Every evening during the voyage Mr. Mopski and the dinosaurs sang
songs from the old country. They sang "Hush, Hush, Little Cockroach," and
"The River Dluda Is Flowing Backwards," and "The Tzar's Third Son Has
Only Ten Toes," and many others.

Finally, the boat landed and the crates were sent to Paris. Soon the skeletons were
on display in the Musée des dinosaurs.

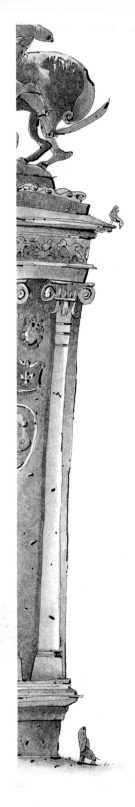

Everyone came to see them. Socialites, professors, beautiful models, and antique dealers clustered around the enormous beasts. Mr. Mopski watched the bones very carefully.

"How do you like Paris?" Mr. Mopski asked.

"They have funny accents," the tricerosaurus mumbled.

"We all do," replied Mr. Mopski.

"But I love to watch them going in and out of the *métro*," the stegatops said. "Such a bustle!"

The tricerosaurus had been set up to face the Eiffel Tower. "What do you think of that?" Mr. Mopski asked him.

"It's interesting," the tricerosaurus admitted. "It reminds me of the backbones of icthyosaurus skeletons." Then he sighed. "But I miss my beautiful park, back at our own museum."

"You are in the world's most beautiful city," Mr. Mopski told him.

"It's not the same thing," the tricerosaurus insisted.

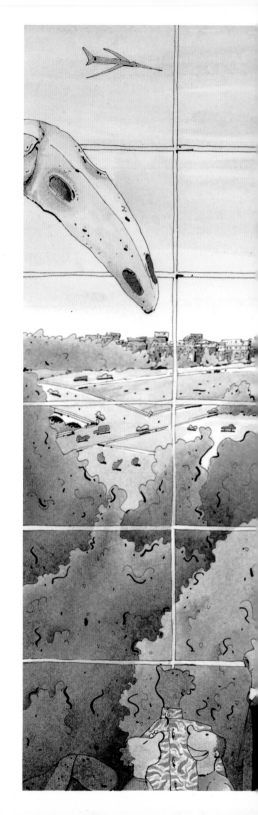

He cheered up when he and the stegatops were crated up again and were sent to Florence. "It will be a change," he remarked.

The dinosaurs were put on display in the Palazzo Vecchio. Peddlers of ornamental leather goods set up their stalls beside the palace entrance. Some sneaked in and unfolded trays of green leather, which they claimed was genuine dinosaur skin, before the police drove them away. Artists set up their easels at every angle around the bones.

Every afternoon, nuns in wide white hats led in lines of schoolboys who listened to accounts of these marvelous creatures. Mr. Mopski kept a close watch. On the third day an angelic-looking boy drew a charcoal moustache on the stegatops.

The stegatops grumbled when Mr. Mopski scrubbed off the moustache that evening. "Couldn't I keep it?" he pleaded. "It makes me look more up-to-date."

"No one would believe it's the real you," warned the tricerosaurus.

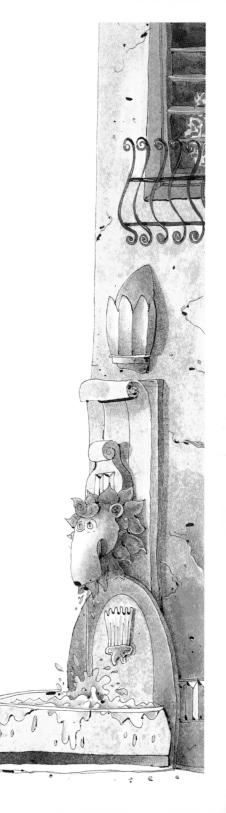

The following week the dinosaurs were sent to London. Both were happy in the Imperial Museum, surrounded by great relief carvings from Nineveh and giant statues of ancient kings.

"This is how people *should* look," the stegatops remarked. Both dinosaurs ignored, as well as they could, the astonished crowds who stood gawking at them.

The Rolling Bones set up amplifiers and guitars near the skeletons to play at lunch hour. At first, the stegatops enjoyed the vibrations; the tricerosaurus was skeptical. After the third day, both dinosaurs told Mr. Mopski that their bones were starting to fall apart. Fortunately, someone tied the rock group's wires in such a complicated knot that, by the time they were untied, the musicians had to leave for a concert at Stonehenge.

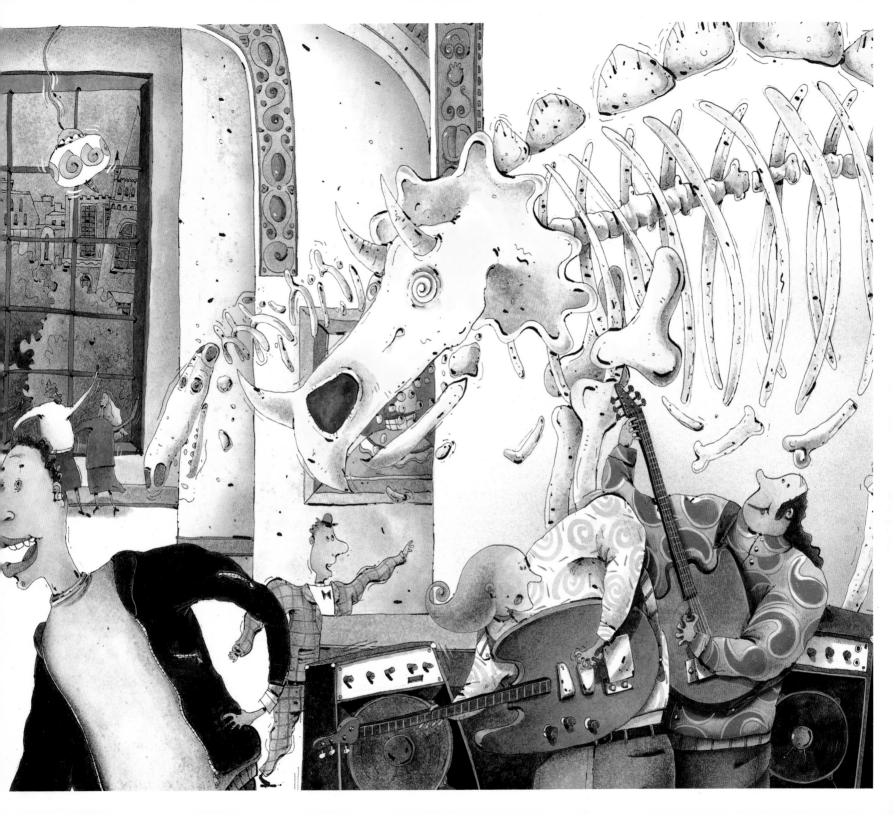

Despite the new sights, the dinosaurs seemed sad. To cheer them up, Mr. Mopski sang "The Schoolmaster's Bicycle," which is impossible to sing without laughing aloud. But even this did not make them happy.

"What in the world is wrong?" he asked.

"We're homesick," said the tricerosaurus.

"Yes," the stegatops added. "We miss our old museum."

"The hissing radiators," said the tricerosaurus dreamily. "They were like steaming hot springs."

"The drafts when they open the main doors," the stegatops mused, "were like the wind over the ferns."

The tricerosaurus gave a rattling sigh. "I even miss the crowds and the taxis and the schoolchildren. At least they were *our* taxis and *our* schoolchildren."

"I wouldn't mind looking at the old park again," the stegatops admitted. "There was more to see than I gave that park credit for: there were birds and balloons and sometimes band-concerts."

Then both dinosaurs said together, "We want to go home!"

Much troubled, Mr. Mopski turned off the light and went out through the foggy, slippery streets of London to consider the matter in a local pub. When he came back to the museum later in the evening, he was smiling happily.

That night, very late, Mr. Mopski again took out his screwdriver. Quickly, he undid the heads of the dinosaurs; with the utmost skill, he fastened them to the original skeletons. When the crowds came in the next morning, they looked as if they had been cheated.

"A stegosaurus!" one person cried.

"A triceratops!" called another. "What is so special about these? We have better dinosaurs here. Send them back to where they came from!"

The board of directors held an emergency meeting. They sniffed and said, "Send the vulgar beasts back!"

So, by the next train and the next boat, the stegosaurus and the triceratops were shipped back to their own museum.

Mr. Mopski suggested to the directors that the dinosaurs should be put on stands equipped with wheels so they could be moved easily around the Dinosaur Gallery. "That way," he explained, "people can see them in different settings."

He didn't tell them that the dinosaurs also wanted to see different views of the world from time to time, but that was exactly what happened.

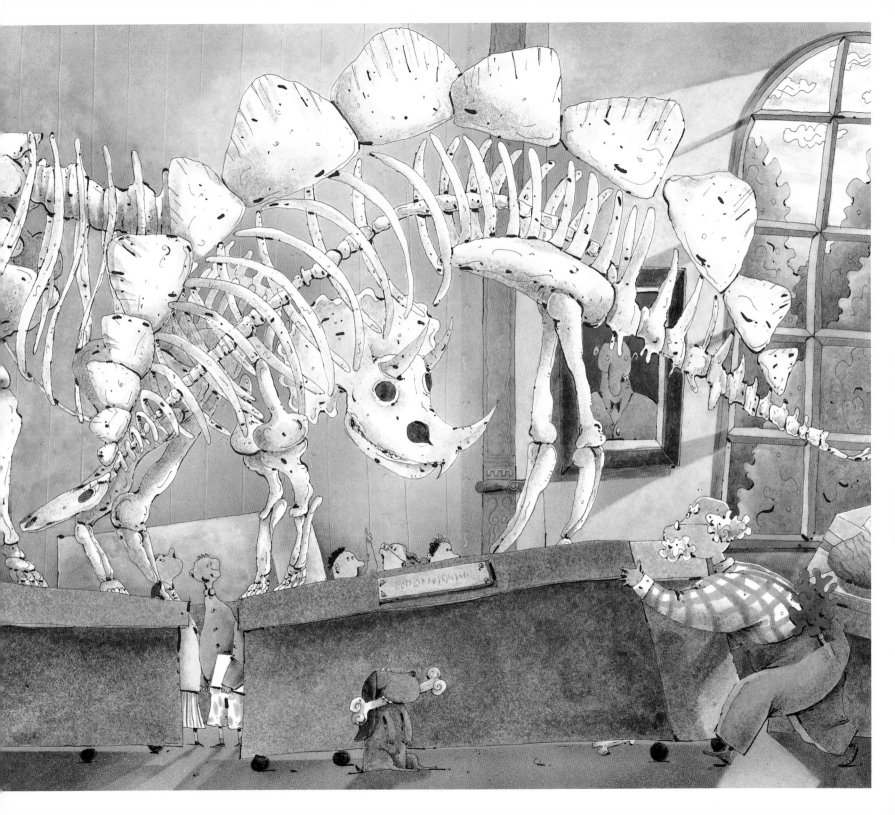

If you should walk by the museum at night and hear strange songs in three voices, only one of which is human, you will know it is the dinosaur duster and his friends singing songs from their distant homeland and talking about all that has happened in the museum, in the busy street, and in the quiet park.

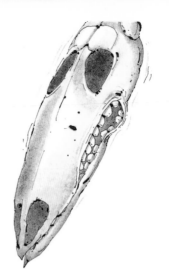